E
MAH

For Oscar, from Marg and Baxter-the-dog (bow-wow!)
—M.M.

For Rose, with love—S.G.

Dashing Dog!
Text copyright © 2002 by Margaret Mahy
Illustrations copyright © 2002 by Sarah Garland
First American edition published in 2002 by Greenwillow Books, an imprint of HarperCollins Publishers.
Published simultaneously in Great Britain by Frances Lincoln Limited.
All rights reserved.
www.harperchildrens.com

A VANESSA HAMILTON BOOK
Designed by Paul Welti
Manufactured in Singapore by Imago Publishing Ltd.

Library of Congress Cataloging-in-Publication Data:
Mahy, Margaret.
Dashing dog! / by Margaret Mahy ; illustrated by Sarah Garland.
p.   cm.
"Greenwillow Books."
Summary: A dashing dog, brushed-up-and-downery, dare-devil-daring and dog-about-townery dog,
is twirled around, ruffled and scuffled and wobbled and whirled around.
ISBN 0-06-000456-8 (trade). ISBN 0-06-000457-6 (lib. bdg.)
[1. Dogs—Fiction. 2. Stories in rhyme.] I. Garland, Sarah, ill. II. Title.
PZ8.3.M278 Das 2002   [E]—dc21 2001033273

10 9 8 7 6 5 4 3 2 1
First American Edition

DASHING DOG!

Margaret Mahy

illustrated by
Sarah Garland

GREENWILLOW BOOKS
An Imprint of HarperCollinsPublishers

Dashing dog! Dashing dog! Oh, what a sight to see!
Cleaned up and curlicued! What a delight to be

Greeting a dog that is brushed-up-and-downery,
Dare-devil-daring, and dog-about-townery.

Seen with a dog that is dapper and dandified,
We'll appear glorious, gallant, and grandified.
What a dog! What a dog! Fit to inspire us all.
Let us go walking, so folk can admire us all.

Down on the sand gulls perambulate, pondering,

Keeping one eye on whatever comes wandering.

Off goes the dog, keen to catch every quill of them.
Up go the gulls, every feather and bill of them.

Sandy and sticky, and cock-a-hoop capery,
Tangled in seaweed by way of a drapery,
Straggling and salty, and spotted and sandified,
Somehow our dog is no longer so dandified.

Breakers are bounding! The breezes are sighing past.
Out of the sand dunes a Frisbee comes flying past.

Horrors! Our dog has leaped up and is catching it,
Seizing it, scrounging it, stealing it, snatching it.

Three other dogs think our dog has done wrong to them,

Sure that the Frisbee should really belong to them.

All in a moment, our darling is twirled around,
Ruffled and scruffled and wobbled and whirled around.

Never mind! Never mind! He's still respectable.
Some of the damage is quite undetectable.

Brush off that seaweed and make him all orderly,
Then we will stroll along, dreamy and dawdle-y.

Dreamy and dawdle-y? Oh, look at that, my dear!
Snooping through sea grass is somebody's cat, I fear.

Horrors! He's seen it! He's off like a thunderbolt.
Trouble-quick, double-quick, devil-dog-dunderbolt.

Into a briar rose, all rambling and riotous –
Wind whistles! Thistles seem ready to fly at us!
Sea grass and bracken and broom may be bearable.
Dog in a briar rose? The damage is terrible.

Wind on the jetty blows out like a gale to sea.
Where's baby Betty? Oh, how could we fail to see!

We were distracted, our little one bumbled off,
Right down the jetty! And *splash*! She has tumbled off.

Run! How we run! But a comet goes ripping past,
Rushing and racing and speedily skipping past,

Diving and dipping where Betty is floundering,
Saving our girl from the danger of drowndering!

Hurrah for the hero who swims, full of cheer, to us,
Bringing back Betty, so precious and dear to us!

Out on the jetty we're towing, then tugging them,
Petting and patting and holding and hugging them.

Look at him walking there – docile and dutiful,
Draggling and dripping . . . but utterly beautiful.
Look at that wagging tail, wet, every bend of it.
But he's our HERO – and that is the end of it.